Earthquakes

Ted O'Hare

Bethany, Missouri

Photo Credits:
Cover © William Walsh; Title Page © Adam Dubrowa; Pages 5, 9, 19, 22 © AUSAID/ Gregory Takats; Pages 7,
12 © USGS; Page 13 © USGS/ Dan Dzurisin, Fema/ Kevin Galvin; Page 15 © Fema/ Marty Bahamonde,
AUSAID/ Gregory Takats; Page 17 © FEMA, Library of Congress; Page 21 © FEMA

Cataloging-in-Publication Data

O'Hare, Ted, 1961-
    Earthquakes / Ted O'Hare. — 1st ed.
    p. cm. — (Natural disasters)

    Includes bibliographical references and index.
    Summary: Illustrations and text introduce earthquakes,
from their history and causes, to how they are measured
and where they occur.
    ISBN-13: 978-1-4242-1400-6 (lib. bdg. : alk. paper)
    ISBN-10: 1-4242-1400-9 (lib. bdg. : alk. paper)
    ISBN-13: 978-1-4242-1490-7 (pbk. : alk. paper)
    ISBN-10: 1-4242-1490-4 (pbk. : alk. paper)

    1. Earthquakes—Juvenile literature. [1. Earthquakes.
2. Natural disasters.] I. O'Hare, Ted, 1961- II. Title.
III. Series.
    QE521.3.O43 2007
    551.2'2—dc22

First edition
© 2007 Fitzgerald Books
802 N. 41st Street, P.O. Box 505
Bethany, MO 64424, U.S.A.
Printed in China
Library of Congress Control Number: 2006940868

Table of Contents

What Makes an Earthquake?

An earthquake happens when there is strong movement of the Earth's surface. This is usually caused by rock inside the Earth as it shifts and moves.

The land may move, starting **landslides** and causing buildings to crumble. Many people are left homeless, and some may even be killed.

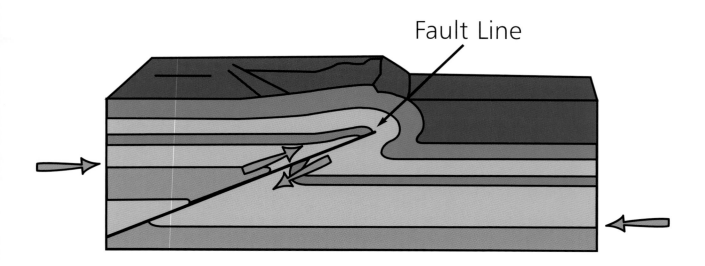

Fault Line

There are many small earthquakes every day. People don't even feel them. But some are strong and cause lots of damage.

An earthquake can occur anywhere. There are some places where earthquakes happen a lot. This is because of cracks in the Earth's crust known as **faults**.

7

An earthquake can happen under water. The result is sometimes a powerful wave known as a **tsunami**.

In 2004 a terrible tsunami hit areas around the Indian Ocean. It was the result of an undersea earthquake. As many as 280,000 people died.

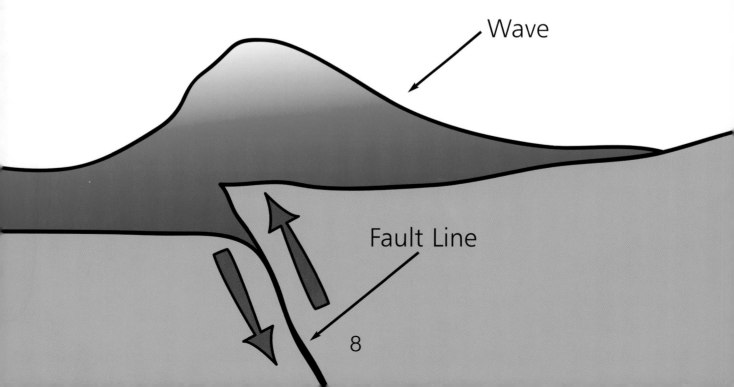

Wave

Fault Line

8

9

The Earth is made up of three layers. The outer layer is called the **crust**. It is made up of rock sections, which move slowly. These sections are known as **tectonic plates**.

The **mantle** is the Earth's middle layer. This is made up of hot rock called **magma**. The **core** is the layer close to the Earth's center.

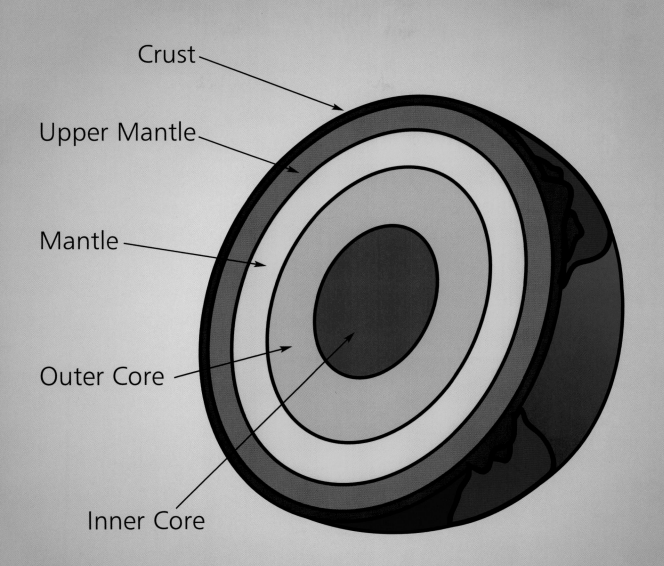

Crust

Upper Mantle

Mantle

Outer Core

Inner Core

Studying Earthquakes

Some scientists learn about earthquakes by studying them. These people are known as **seismologists**. They study the time, strength, and duration of an earthquake.

They learn where the heart of the earthquake is. This is known as its **epicenter**, and it is usually where the heaviest damage occurs.

Measuring Earthquakes

The Richter Scale is the best-known way to measure the strength of an earthquake. Used first in 1935, the scale is named after a seismologist, Charles Richter. The higher the number, the more powerful the earthquake.

The Richter Scale

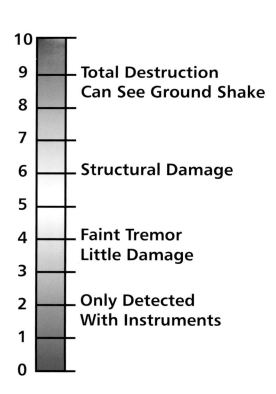

California Earthquakes

Much of California lies on top of a fault line, known as the San Andreas Fault. Earthquakes happen a lot in California.

In 1906 a famous earthquake struck San Francisco. The quake was bad enough, but fire occurred, causing further damage. In 1989 another major quake struck San Francisco. And in 1994 a quake hit the Los Angeles area.

Famous Earthquakes

In 1556 an earthquake struck China. More than 830,000 people died as a result of this terrible earthquake.

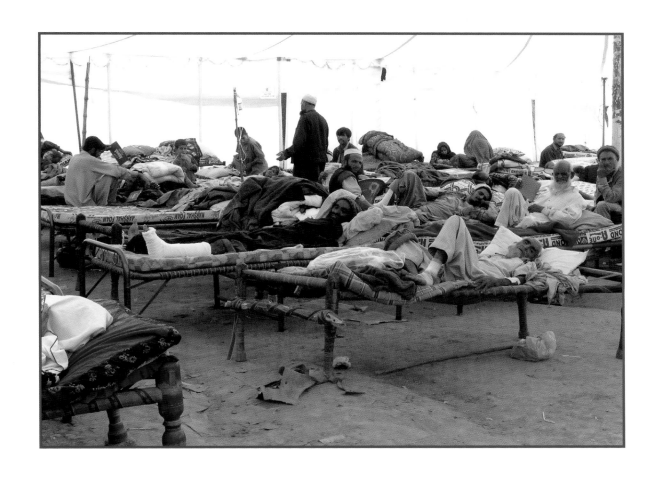

A large quake struck Pakistan in 2005. It measured 7.6 on the Richter Scale. People all over the world sent help to the victims.

When Disaster Strikes

No one can prevent earthquakes. They will always occur.

People are building stronger buildings that will survive earthquakes. They are also building safer roads and overpasses in places with a lot of earthquakes.

Scientists are trying to learn more about how and when earthquakes strike. With better information, they may be able to give advance warning. This could help save people when an earthquake strikes.

Glossary

core (KORR) — the Earth's hot center

crust (KRUST) — the Earth's hard outer layer

epicenter (EP uh sen tur) — the center of an earthquake

faults (FAWLTZ) — cracks in the Earth's crust

landslides (LAND slydz) — movement of land often caused by an earthquake

magma (MAG muh) — melted rock under the Earth's surface

mantle (MANT ul) — the layer of earth between the crust and the core

seismologists (size MOHL uh jistz) — scientists who study earthquakes

tectonic plates (tek TAWN ik PLAYTZ) — pieces of the Earth's crust

tsunami (soo NAHM ee) — a large sea wave often caused by an underwater earthquake

Index

FURTHER READING

DK Publishing. *Volcanoes and Earthquakes (Eyewitness)*. DK Children's Books, 2004.

Prager, Ellen J. *Jump into Science: Earthquakes*. National Geographic Children's Books, 2002.

Simon, Seymour. *Earthquakes*. HarperCollins, 2006.

WEBSITES TO VISIT

Because Internet links change so often, Fitzgerald Books has developed an online list of websites related to the subject of this book. This site is updated regularly. Please use this link to access the list: www.fitzgeraldbookslinks.com/nd/ear

ABOUT THE AUTHOR

Ted O'Hare is an author and editor of children's nonfiction books. Ted has written over fifty children's books over the past decade. Ted has worked for many publishing houses including the Macmillan Children's Book Group.